YOUR PET CAT

A TRUE BOOK

by

Elaine Landau

Children's Press®
A Division of Grolier Publishing

New York London Hong Kong Sydney
Danbury, Connecticut

A cat balances
on a fence.

Reading Consultant
Linda Cornwell
Learning Resource Consultant
Indiana Department
of Education

Author's Dedication:
For Jerry, Bianca,
and Abraham

Library of Congress Cataloging-in-Publication Data

Landau, Elaine
    Your pet cat / by Elaine Landau.
        p.   cm. — (A True book)
    Includes bibliographical references and index.
    Summary: A simple introduction to choosing and caring for a pet cat.
    ISBN 0-516-20381-9 (lib.bdg.)   0-516-26260-2 (pbk.)
    1. Cats—Juvenile literature. [1. Cats. 2. Pets] I. Title. II. Series.
SF445.7.L34 1997
636.8'083—dc21   97–15626
                                                                        CIP
                                                                        AC

Contents

Cats love human company.

Cats as Pets

Forget all the bad things you've heard about cats. They are not loners or stuck-up. They are not finicky eaters. Black cats don't bring bad luck.

The truth is that cats make terrific pets. In fact, they are the most popular pets in the United States. Cats are great

Cats can live comfortably indoors—even in small apartments.

companions, and they love human company. They are small enough to live comfortably in an apartment or small house, and they are very clean.

Cats need far less care than dogs. You won't have to walk your cat twice a day in the freezing cold or blistering heat. However, when you bring home a cat you are taking on a big responsibility. There's more to being a cat owner than just putting out food and water for

Cats are the most popular pets in the United States.

your pet each day. It will be up to you to give your cat the care and love it needs. Responsible pet owners make time for their animals— even when they would rather be doing something else.

Think it over. Are you ready to do what it takes? A pet is a wonderful living thing; treat it accordingly.

Caring for a cat is a big responsibility.

Picking Out Your Cat

Before you choose your cat, you'll have to decide whether you want a pedigree or a mixed-breed cat.

Pedigrees come from a long line of purebred cats. They are bred to have specific traits or characteristics. Many people prefer a certain type of pedi-

The cat on the left is a pedigree Maine Coon cat. The cat above is a mixed breed.

gree cat, such as a Siamese or a Persian. But these animals cost a lot more than mixed-breed cats. Also, pedigree cats tend to have more health problems than mixed breeds.

Mixed-breed cats are available at animal shelters.

Most pedigree cats are sold by breeders. Mixed-breed cats are available free or inexpensively from your local animal shelter or humane society.

When you choose a pet, look for a healthy animal. A

Look for an active and playful cat.

kitten should be active and playful. Healthy kittens and full-grown cats have bright, clear eyes.

The cat's nose, mouth, and ears should be clean. Look

Healthy cats have bright, clear eyes.

carefully at an animal that keeps scratching its ears or shaking its head. These may be signs that the cat has mites or an infection.

A cat's coat should be soft and smooth with no bald spots. Don't bring home a cat that has rough spots, scabs, or wounds.

Cat Naps

Cats sleep a lot. In fact, they spend about two-thirds to three-quarters of the day sleeping. That's more than any other mammal! No one really knows why, but any time, day or night, can be nap time for a cat.

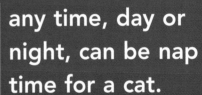

Your Cat's Veterinarian

Soon after bringing your new pet home, take it to a veterinarian. Your veterinarian will check your cat's general health.

Proper care will help keep your pet in good health. But even healthy cats need regular visits to the veterinarian. Your cat needs vaccinations to

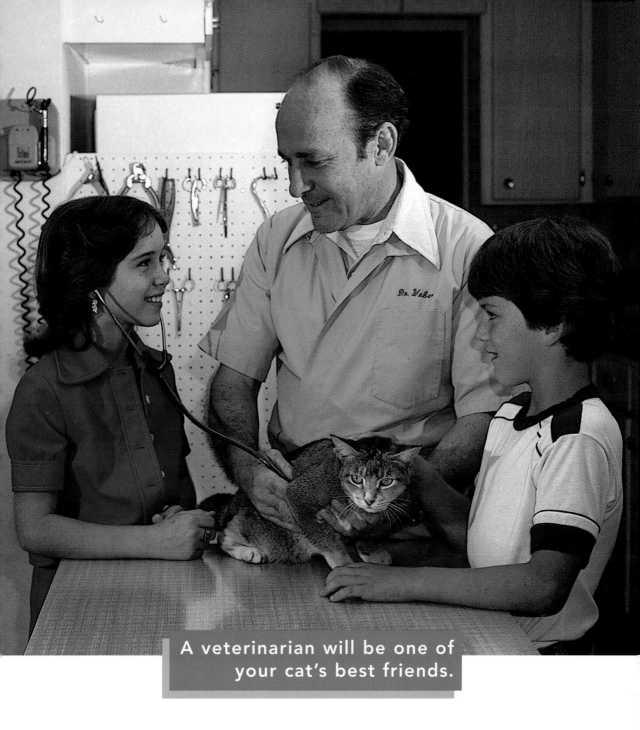

A veterinarian will be one of
your cat's best friends.

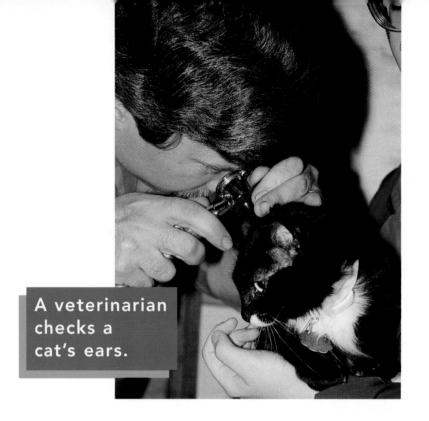

A veterinarian checks a cat's ears.

protect it against diseases. The veterinarian will also check and treat your cat for internal parasites. These are small creatures, such as tapeworms or roundworms, that live inside the animal and can make it sick.

The Litter Box

Every new cat owner will need some basic supplies. One of the most important of these is the litter box, which you should set up before you bring your pet home.

The litter box will be your cat's bathroom. Pet stores carry many different types of litter

Choose a litter
box that is easy
to clean.

boxes. Some are covered, some are uncovered, and some look like houses.

Pick one that is easy to clean, and fill it with a layer of kitty litter about 1½ to 2 inches (3½ to 5 cm) deep. You can buy a deodorizing litter that will help keep the box smelling fresh. However, litter that is too heavily scented may offend your cat's sense of smell.

Use a litter scoop to remove wet and soiled litter from the box twice a day. Empty the litter box once a week, and wash it out with hot, soapy water. Avoid bleach or harsh detergents, and always rinse the box well. Then dry it thoroughly, add fresh litter, and return the box to its usual place.

Keep the litter box where your cat can easily find it. Don't pick a busy, well-traveled spot in the house for the box. Also, try to keep it away from the areas where your cat eats or sleeps.

Cat Food

Many different cat foods are available. Cats need different types of food at different stages of their lives.

Whether you select a dry, semi-moist, or canned food depends on your cat. When you first bring your cat home, continue feeding it the type of

Ask your veterinarian
to recommend
food for your cat.

food it has been eating. Then ask your veterinarian to recommend the best food for your pet.

Never suddenly change an animal's diet unless your veterinarian recommends it. Instead, gradually mix the new food with the old. Use a little more of the new food each day until the switch is completed.

Feed your cat at the same time in the same place each day. Cats like routines, and this way you can be sure your pet's food

is fresh. Leaving food out all day encourages some cats to overeat. And in warm weather, some foods may spoil. Make sure that fresh water is always available for your cat, and change its water at least once a day.

Do not feed your pet table scraps or treats intended for humans. Unfortunately, most cats love these foods—and even beg for them. But they can be harmful to the animal over time.

Many human foods are too high in fat for a cat. And what may seem like a small amount to you is really quite a lot for a cat or kitten. Never give your cat bones. Many cats have choked to death on bones.

Caring For Your Cat

All cats need to scratch and sharpen their claws regularly. Get your pet a scratching post to save your family's furniture, rugs, and curtains. You can't stop a cat from scratching, but you can try to teach it what to scratch.

A cat will scratch
carpets and furniture
if they don't have a
scratching post.

Cats may have trouble seeing the difference between a carpet and a carpet-covered scratching post.

The scratching post should have a rough surface that your cat will want to sink its claws into. Posts that are covered with rope are excellent.

Avoid carpet-covered scratching posts, though. Your pet may not know the difference between the carpet on the post and the one on your floor!

Make sure the scratching post is sturdy and won't easily tip over. It should also be tall enough to allow the cat to stretch its body while it's scratching. Full-grown cats often won't use a post that is too short.

Cats are naturally clean animals. They wash themselves with their tongues throughout the day, and most cats love to be brushed, or groomed.

Brushing helps keep your cat healthy. It removes dead hair from your animal's coat so that it swallows less hair when it washes itself.

Short-haired cats that live indoors need to be brushed about once a week. Use a good grooming brush. Long-haired cats should be brushed

Cats groom them-selves frequently (above). Most cats love to be brushed (right), and it's good for them.

every day. And once a week, their fur should also be combed with a grooming comb. Combing helps keep their fur from becoming matted.

Feline Fun

Just like you, cats don't like to be bored. Keep your cat happy and active with toys. Ping-Pong balls make good toys, and small plastic balls with bells inside are also favorites.

Cats love soft toy mice or birds, but avoid toys that have sharp edges or glued-on parts. And make sure that any toys you buy won't break apart. Cats have been known to choke on small pieces and bells.

You can also find playthings for your cat around the house. They love to pounce on balls of crumpled paper. They also like cardboard boxes, wooden thread spools, or just a big paper bag. Be creative and you'll save money.

You and Your Cat

Before long, you and your cat will be best buddies. The following tips will help you keep your new pal healthy and happy.

Cuddle and pet your cat, but don't overdo it. Cats need love, but they also need rest and time alone. Being a

Cats need cuddling (left) but they also need time alone (below).

Some houseplants can harm cats—and some cats can harm houseplants!

responsible cat owner means paying attention to your pet's feelings. Learn to identify and respect your cat's needs.

Keep houseplants where your cat can't reach them. Many cats love to dig in houseplant soil and even chew on leaves. This can be very dangerous because some houseplants are poisonous to cats.

Keep all chemicals and household cleaning fluids in

cabinets that lock or close tightly. Make sure your cat can't get to them. Such accidents have sometimes been deadly.

Cats love to look out at the world through windows. They enjoy watching the cars and the people passing by. Clear off at least one windowsill for your cat. A window with a tree in front of it is ideal. Cats especially enjoy watching birds and squirrels. But first

Cats love looking at the world through a window.

check to see that your windows or screens close tightly. Cats don't really have nine lives.

Congratulations on choosing a cat as a pet. The two of you are about to begin a wonderful journey of friendship and fun. Enjoy yourselves!

Your cat will be a great friend.

To Find Out More

Here are some additional resources to help you learn more about cats:

 **Books**

Barnett, Norman S. **Cats.** Franklin Watts, 1990

Cole, Joanna. **My New Kitten.** Morrow Junior Books, 1995.

Evans, Mark. **Kitten.** Dorling Kindersley, 1992.

Jessel, Camilla. **The Kitten Book.** Candlewick Press, 1992.

Mattern, Joanne, **A Picture Book of Cats.** Troll Associates, 1991.

Parsons, Alexandra. **Amazing Cats.** Knopf, 1990.

Peterson-Fleming, Judy. **Kitten Care and Critters, Too!** Tambourine Books, 1994.

Ryden, Hope. **Your Cat's Wild Cousins.** Lodestar Books, 1992.

💡 Organizations and Online Sites

Acme Pet

http://www.acmepet.com/

Includes useful information on cats including tips on choosing a cat, finding a breeder, grooming, and general care.

American Cat Fanciers Association (ACFA)

P.O. Box 203
Point Lookout, MO 65726
Phone: (417) 334-5430
http://www.acfacat.com/

This organization promotes interest in all domesticated, purebred, and non-pure-bred cats.

American Society for the Prevention of Cruelty to Animals (ASPCA)

424 East 92nd Street
New York, NY 10128-6804
(212) 876-7700, ext. 4421
http://www.aspca.org/

This organization is dedicated to the prevention of cruelty to animals. It also provides advice and services for caring for all kinds of animals.

Cat Fanciers' Association

1805 Atlantic Avenue
P.O. Box 1005
Manasquan, NJ 08736
(908) 528-9797
http://www.cfainc.org/cfa/

The world's largest registry of pedigreed cats. The Web site includes information on cat shows, cat breeds, and cat care.

Cat Fanciers Web Site

http://www.fanciers.com/

Provides general information about cats and cat care, and includes breed descriptions.

rec.pets.cats FAQ Homepage

http://WWW.Zmall.Com/ pet/cat-faqs/

This Web site includes lists of questions and answers about cats and cat care.

45

Important Words

breeder person who mates cats to produce a specific breed of cat

deodorizing litter litter that eliminates foul odors

detergent chemical substance used for cleaning

humane society charitable organization dedicated to the protection of animals

mites tiny animals that live on other animals; related to ticks

parasite animal or plant that lives off another living thing

pedigree descended from a line of purebred cats

vaccination the injection of a substance that protects an animal from a specific disease

veterinarian doctor who treats animals

Index

(**Boldface** page numbers indicate illustrations.)

Meet the Author

Elaine Landau worked as a newspaper reporter, children's book editor, and youth services librarian before becoming a full time writer. She has written more than ninety books for young people.

Ms. Landau lives in Florida with her husband and son.